The Outside Dog

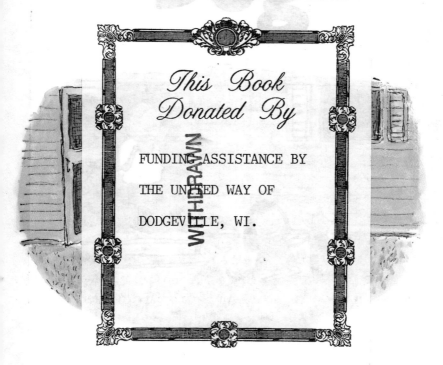

This Book
Donated By

FUNDING ASSISTANCE BY

THE UNITED WAY OF

DODGEVILLE, WI.

story by Charlotte Pomerantz

pictures by Jennifer Plecas

HarperTrophy
A Division of HarperCollinsPublishers

For Flora Cass Gosch

— C. P.

I Can Read Book is a registered trademark of HarperCollins Publishers.

The Outside Dog
Text copyright © 1993 by Charlotte Pomerantz
Illustrations copyright © 1993 by Jennifer Plecas
Printed in the United States of America. All rights reserved.

Library of Congress Cataloging-in-Publication Data
Pomerantz, Charlotte.
The outside dog / story by Charlotte Pomerantz ; pictures by Jennifer
Plecas.
p. cm. (An I can read book)
Summary: Marisol, who lives in Puerto Rico, wants a dog very much but
her grandfather will not let her have one, until a skinny mutt wins him over.
ISBN 0-06-024782-7. — ISBN 0-06-024783-5 (lib. bdg.)
ISBN 0-06-444187-3 (pbk.)
[1. Dogs—Fiction. 2. Grandfathers—Fiction 3. Puerto Rico—Fiction.]
I. Plecas, Jennifer, ill. II. Title. III. Series.
PZ7.P77Ou 1993   91-6351
[E]—dc20   CIP
                                                                AC

First Harper Trophy edition, 1995.

Contents

Spanish words in the story:

Doña	*(DON-ya)*	Madame
Colmado	*(col-MA-doe)*	Grocery store
Vete	*(VEH-tay)*	Scram
Abuelito	*(ab-wel-EE-toe)*	Grandpa
Qué raro	*(kay RA-ro)*	How strange
¿Entiendes?	*(en-TYEN-days)*	Understand?
Qué cosa	*(kay KO-sa)*	My goodness
Lo vi	*(lo VEE)*	I saw him
¿Qué pasa?	*(kay PA-sa)*	What's the matter?

Marisol Wants a Dog

Marisol lived with her grandfather
in Puerto Rico.
Their home was in a little village
on the side of a hill.
There was a big mango tree
in the yard,
and mountains all around.
Below, was the warm blue sea.

Their neighbor up the hill
was Doña Elvira.
She owned a little *colmado*,
where they bought their groceries.

6

Their neighbor down the hill
was a fisherman named Nando.
Sometimes, in the early morning,
Marisol went fishing with him.

There were many dogs on the hill.

They were strays.

No one owned or took care of them

Marisol had always wanted a dog,
but Grandfather said they had fleas
and ticks and who knows what.
Whenever a dog came into the yard,
Grandfather chased it away.
"*¡Vete!*" he yelled. "Scram!"

One day, Grandfather and Marisol
came home and found a dog
sitting near their house.
He was a skinny brown mutt
with perky ears and big brown eyes.

10

Grandfather chased him away.

But that evening, the dog came back.

When Marisol thought

her grandfather was not looking,

she sneaked out and petted him.

"Marisol," said Grandfather,

"I told you not to pet the dogs.

They have fleas and ticks

and who knows what."

"But, *Abuelito*, this one does not,"

said Marisol. "Look!"

"*¡Qué raro!*" Grandfather said.

"There is not a flea on him."

"So may I pet him?" asked Marisol.

"You may pet this one.

But only this one.

And don't feed him a thing!

¿Entiendes?" said Grandfather.

"Once you feed a stray dog,
he never goes away."

13

Later, when they were eating

pork chops and potatoes,

the dog came and sat very quietly

outside the screen door.

"Grandpa, do you think he is hungry?"

asked Marisol.

"Of course he is hungry.

Every stray dog on this hill

is hungry," said Grandfather.

"If I worried about that,

I would be feeding twenty dogs."

15

Grandfather piled the leftover bones

onto a plate.

"What are you going to do

with the bones?" asked Marisol.

"Throw them in the garbage,

of course," said Grandfather.

"Why don't you give them to the dog?"

asked Marisol.

Grandfather sighed. "All right.

Just this once. But not here.

Out on the road, away from the house.

I don't want him to think

that this is his home."

They walked to the road.

The dog followed.

When Grandfather dumped
the plate of bones,
three other dogs came running.

"Scram!" Grandfather shouted.

"Let this one eat. *¡Vete!*"

A Collar for Pancho

Grandfather sipped dark coffee
in the doorway.

Marisol patted the dog.

"He is sort of nice looking

for a mutt, isn't he, Grandpa?"

"He's okay," said Grandfather.

"I don't think he is all mutt,"
said Marisol.
"Maybe ninety percent.
The rest of him
looks like a fancy dog."

20

"If he is part mutt,

he is all mutt," said Grandfather.

Marisol parted his fur.

"Uh-oh!" she said.

"Now I see a couple of fleas.

We better get him a flea collar."

21

"*¡Qué cosa!*" said Grandfather.

"Whoever heard of putting
a flea collar on a stray dog?"

"Oh, Grandpa, please let me buy one
with the money Uncle Cuco gave me
for my birthday."

Grandfather shrugged.

"I suppose you can buy what you wish
with your own money," he said,
"but don't think
this dog is going to like
having a collar around his neck."

At Doña Elvira's store,

there were flea collars in two sizes:

medium and large.

"Is he a medium dog or a large dog?"

asked Doña Elvira.

"He is sort of medium large,"
said Marisol.

"I think he is more medium
than large," said Grandfather.

Marisol nodded.

"I think so, too," she said.

When they got back to the house,

the dog sat very still while Marisol

put the flea collar on him.

"That's odd," said Grandfather.

"I didn't think he would like it."

"He loves it," said Marisol proudly.

26

At bedtime, Marisol said,
"The dog is in the yard, *Abuelito*.
Is it okay if he sleeps there?"
"I don't see any way to stop him,"
said Grandfather.

"There is a full moon,

so he will not be in the dark,"

said Marisol. "And when it rains,

he can keep dry

under the mango tree."

"Uh-huh," said Grandfather.

'Grandpa! He's asleep!" said Marisol.

'I guess he feels at home,"

;aid Grandfather.

Marisol's eyes brightened. "At home?"

'I didn't say this *was* his home.

  just said he *feels* at home.

Now go to bed," said Grandfather.

"Grandpa!" Marisol called,

"you forgot to kiss me good night."

Marisol heard the floor creak,

as Grandfather got up

and crossed the room

in his bare feet.

"Sleep well, Mari," he said.

Marisol smiled. "That is what I said

when I said good night to Pancho."

"Pancho?" said Grandfather.

"Who is Pancho?"

"My dog," said Marisol.

"I named him Pancho."

The Search

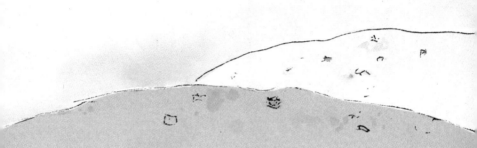

At supper the next day,

they had stew.

There were no leftovers.

Marisol did not say anything,

but Grandfather could see

she was unhappy.

"Give him a little chopped meat
from the refrigerator," he said.

"Does chopped meat cost a lot?"
asked Marisol.

"It costs plenty," said Grandfather.

"Maybe we should get him
some dry dog food," said Marisol.
"I certainly cannot afford
to feed him chopped meat,"
said Grandfather.

35

When they returned from the *colmado*

later that evening,

Grandfather carried the groceries.

Marisol carried a bag of dog food.

But Pancho was not there.

He was not there

when Marisol woke up

the next morning,

nor the morning after that.

"Don't worry," said Grandfather.

"If anything happened to Pancho,

Nando or Doña Elvira would tell us."

38

Marisol ran to talk to Nando
before he went fishing.

"Nando, have you seen Pancho?"

asked Marisol.

"He hasn't been home

for two days and two nights."

"Hmm," said Nando.

"He has probably found

a female dog that he likes."

"You mean Pancho has a girlfriend?"

asked Marisol.

"Why not? He is a healthy young dog.

Come fishing with me, Mari.

The snappers are biting real good.

It will take your mind off the dog."

"No, thanks, Nando," said Marisol.

"I want to speak to Doña Elvira."

41

Inside the *colmado*

it was cool and dark.

"Doña Elvira, have you seen my dog?"

asked Marisol.

"He disappeared two days ago."

"No," said Doña Elvira.

"I have not seen him,

and I *always* notice Pancho."

43

"Pancho may have a female friend,"
said Doña Elvira.

"That's what Nando thinks,"
said Marisol.

Doña Elvira gave Marisol
a lemon drop and a lollypop.

"Take these," she said,

"and don't worry about Pancho."

44

Marisol woke up

in the middle of the night.

She felt her way to the door

and called Pancho's name.

Pancho was not in the yard.

As she walked back to her room,

she bumped into Grandfather.

"Marisol, what are you doing up

in the middle of the night?"

"I was looking for Pancho.

What were *you* doing?"

asked Marisol.

"I was looking for him, too."

Grandfather led her back to bed

and tucked her in.

"I don't know why I love

such a foolish little girl,"

he said.

Marisol looked at him shyly.

"I don't know why I love

such a foolish old grandpa."

Pancho Saves the Day

"Wake up, Marisol. He's back!
Pancho is back!" said Grandfather.
Marisol jumped out of bed
and ran outdoors.
"Pancho!" she cried.
She hugged him again and again.
Grandfather brought out
a big bowl of dog food.

Doña Elvira came running.

"*¡Lo vi!*" she shouted. "I saw him!
I saw Pancho."

50

Just then, Nando came up the hill
with two red snappers.
"Pancho is home!"
Marisol called out.

"Where have you been, Pancho?"

Nando asked.

He knelt down and put his ear

up to the dog's nose.

Nando nodded to the dog

and then stood up.

"It is just as I thought," he said.

"Pancho has a girlfriend."

"What did I tell you,"

said Doña Elvira. "Look at him.

Skinny, chewed up, and worn out."

Marisol kneeled down
and put her ear to the dog's nose,
the way Nando had.
"Are you sure he said that, Nando?
I can't hear anything."

"Nobody can, except Nando,"
said Grandfather.

"That's true," said Doña Elvira.

"Nando is the only one on the hill
who understands dog talk."

That evening,

when Marisol and Grandfather

sat down to dinner,

they heard Pancho barking.

Grandfather got up

to see what was the matter.

There was a pot of rice
burning on the stove.
Pancho was barking
because of the smoke.
"Thanks, Pancho," Grandfather said
and turned off the stove.

"What happened?" asked Marisol.

"Why did you say, 'Thanks, Pancho'?"

"Because," said Grandfather,

"he smelled something burning

and warned us."

"Oh, Grandpa," said Marisol,
"aren't we lucky to have Pancho?
What if he had not been here?"
"We could have had a fire,"
said Grandfather.

At bedtime Marisol was quiet.

"*¿Qué pasa?*" asked Grandfather.

"What's the matter?"

"Nothing. I just wondered

if Pancho really is our dog."

"Marisol," said Grandfather,

"I told you from the start

that once you feed a dog,

he thinks you own him."

"Do we own him?" asked Marisol.

Grandfather chuckled.

"I don't know," he said.

"But he sure owns us."

"Does that mean

we will always feed him?"

"I guess so," said Grandfather.

"He is a good watchdog."

Marisol hugged Grandfather.

"I love you, *Abuelito,*" said Marisol.

"I love you, too, Mari.

But remember,

Pancho is an outside dog.

And he will always be

an outside dog."

"Of course," said Marisol.

"I have always wanted

an outside dog."